JuLiuS

CHOCOLATE CHIPS

STORY BY AngeLA JohnSon

PiCTURES BY DAV PiLKeY

SCHOLASTIC INC.
New York Toronto London Auckland Sydney

ISBN 0-590-63535-2

Text copyright © 1993 by Angela Johnson. Illustrations copyright © 1993 by Dav Pilkey.
All rights reserved. Published by Scholastic Inc.,
555 Broadway, New York, NY 10012, by arrangement with Orchard Books.
TRUMPET and the TRUMPET logo are registered trademarks of Scholastic Inc.

12 11 10 9 8 7 6 5 4 3 2 1   7 8 9/9 0 1 2/0

Printed in the U.S.A.   14

First Scholastic printing, January 1997

Book design by Mina Greenstein. The text of this book is set in 18 point Barcelona Bold.
The illustrations are acrylic, watercolor, fabric, instant coffee, crayon, and india ink
reproduced in full color.

To Ashley,
who loves the music too

Maya's granddaddy lived in Alabama,
but wintered in Alaska.

He told Maya that was the reason he
liked ice cubes in his coffee.

On one of Granddaddy's visits from Alaska, he brought a crate.

A surprise for Maya!

"Something that will teach you fun and sharing." Granddaddy smiled. "Something for my special you."

Maya hoped it was a horse or an older
brother.
She'd always wanted one or the other.

But it was a pig.

A big pig.
An Alaskan pig, who did a polar bear
imitation and climbed out of the crate.

Julius had come.

Maya's parents didn't think that they
would like Julius.
He showed them no fun, no sharing.

Maya loved Julius, though, so he stayed.

There never was enough food in the
house after Julius came to stay.
He slurped coffee and ate too much
peanut butter.

He would roll himself in flour when he
wanted Maya to bake him cookies.

Julius made big messes and spread the newspaper everywhere before anyone could read it.

He left crumbs on the sheets and never picked up his towels.

Julius made too much noise.
He'd stay up late watching old movies,

and he'd always play records when
everybody else wanted to read.

But Maya knew the other Julius too. . . .

The Julius who was fun to take on walks 'cause he did great dog imitations and chased cats.

The Julius who sneaked into stores
with her and tried on clothes.
Julius liked anything blue and stretchy.

They'd try on hats too.
Maya liked red felt.
Julius liked straw—it tasted better.

Trying on shoes was hard, though. . . .

Julius would swing for hours on the playground with Maya.

He'd protect her from the scary things
at night too . . . sometimes.

**Maya loved the Julius who taught her
how to dance to jazz records . . .**

and eat peanut butter from the jar, without
getting any on the ceiling.

Maya didn't think all the older brothers
in the world could have taught her that.

Julius loved the Maya who taught him
that even though he was a pig he didn't
have to act like he lived in a barn.

Julius didn't think all the Alaskan pigs
in the world could have taught him that.

Maya shared the things she'd learned
from Julius with her friends.
Swinging . . .

trying on hats, and dancing to jazz records.

Julius shared the things Maya had
taught him with her parents . . . sometimes.

And that was all right, because living
with Maya and sharing everything
was even better than being a cool pig
from Alaska.